Alien Island

Story by Michael Pryor

Illustrations by Vincent Batignole

Alien Island

Text: Michael Pryor
Publishers: Tania Mazzeo and Eliza Webb
Series consultant: Amanda Sutera
Hands on Heads Consulting
Editor: Jess Mackay
Project editor: Annabel Smith
Designer: Jess Kelly
Project designer: Danielle Maccarone
Illustrations: Vincent Batignole
Production controller: Renee Tome

NovaStar

ISBN 978 0 17 033503 4

Cengage Learning Australia
Level 5, 80 Dorcas Street
Southbank VIC 3006 Australia
Phone: 1300 790 853
Email: aust.nelsonprimary@cengage.com

For learning solutions, visit **cengage.com.au**

Printed in China by 1010 Printing International Ltd
1 2 3 4 5 6 7 29 28 27 26 25

Nelson acknowledges the Traditional Owners and Custodians of the lands of all First Nations Peoples. We pay respect to Elders past and present, and extend that respect to all First Nations Peoples today.

Contents

Chapter 1

Mars

Skeet hated Mars dust. It got everywhere: in her home, in her hair, in her clothes. She hated it, but she was used to it because she was born and raised on Mars.

Hassan leaned over and nearly put his nose to the window of the school bus. "Wow! Look at that!"

Skeet rolled her eyes. "I have. I did. It's the same as the *last* Atmosphere Generator."

Hassan couldn't take his eyes off the huge machine. "It's so big," he breathed.

That was true. The Atmosphere Generator was a vast complex of pipes, chimneys, lights and vents about a kilometre in circumference and nearly that high.

"I know," Skeet said.

"But did you know that there are thousands of them?" Hassan said. "Thousands scattered across the whole planet, chugging away for more than three hundred years to make a breathable atmosphere for Mars?"

"I do," Skeet said. "Haven't I told you a million times that my great-great-many-great-grandmother was Ingrid Chan, chief engineer of the Mars Terraforming Project?"

Hassan scratched his chin. "Has anyone told you that you exaggerate a lot?"

"Me?" Skeet said. "I'd never exaggerate. Never in a billion years."

Hassan's eyes went wide, and he pointed. "Giraffes!"

Skeet glanced out the window. A herd of giraffes had wandered around the far corner of the Atmosphere Generator. "Giraffes? So? You've been here on Mars for a month and you still get excited by seeing giraffes?"

Hassan's face fell. "Giraffes are extinct on Earth. Just like the elephants and lions and gorillas."

"We had a rhinoceros in our backyard a couple of months ago," Skeet said.

"Wow," Hassan said. "So cool."

"Not really. Earth sounds much cooler."

Hassan shook his head. “Earth is crowded and noisy and dangerous with all the storms and droughts. I’m glad Mum and Dad migrated us to Mars. Mars is great. So much wide open space.”

Skeet shook her head. Mars was boring. Nothing ever happened on Mars. Even this school excursion to see a volcano was going to be dull; she was sure of that. She couldn’t wait to grow up and leave. She wanted to be in the middle of the bright lights of Earth. The showbiz, the history, the celebrities!

“Look!” Hassan pointed. “Eagles!”

Chapter 2

A Cave

Hecates Tholus was one of many volcanoes on Mars, all of them cold and dead. Skeet's class had been studying them, and the end-of-term excursion to Hecates Tholus was meant to be a big treat. Except it was taking forever to get there across the broken, rocky countryside. Even though the bus glided a metre above the surface, Skeet thought it was so slow. Couldn't Ms Budge, their teacher, drive faster than 500 kilometres an hour?

To make things worse, Skeet had been paired up with Hassan, a wide-eyed new Martian. Hassan was always drawing attention to himself, thanks to Mars's gravity only being a third of Earth's.

He was clumsy, he hovered when he walked and his attempts at sports were hilarious. He even had trouble standing up out of his seat. He was quite likely to bounce off the ceiling of the bus, come to think of it.

But Hassan remained cheerful despite all that, Skeet had to admit. It was like his birthday every day.

Eventually, when the bus drew close to a large rocky ridge, Ms Budge slowed down. "We're nearly here," she announced. "Now's the time to remind yourselves about your assignments. And don't forget – always stay with your partner."

Skeet fired up her tablet while Hassan was still fumbling for his. They had to do an ecological survey and record any plants and animals they found, even in the caves that were everywhere in the southern flank of Hecates Tholus. That meant looking closely for insects and moss, to see how the greening of Mars was going.

The ridge extended for kilometres towards the rounded cone of the volcano. The volcano was worn down, streaked reddish brown, and it looked like it had been dormant for a long, long time.

As they climbed down from the bus, Skeet slung her backpack over her shoulder.

Hassan grinned at her. "Where will we start?"

Hassan stared at their surroundings. "Did you know that this whole volcano is nearly two hundred kilometres from side to side?"

Skeet sighed. "Did you know that it's five kilometres high and it's one of the smaller Martian volcanoes?"

"Wow!" Hassan said.

All the other class members had taken spots near the bus. "Come on," Skeet said to Hassan. "Let's find somewhere a bit more interesting."

Skeet skirted a large boulder, then squeezed between a rockfall and some scrubby bushes.

"You think we should be out here?" Hassan said, looking back the way they'd come.

"Relax. Ms Budge said it was okay for us to wander, as long as our tablets have their beacons on."

Hassan peered at his tablet. "I'm double checking."

Skeet pointed. "That's what I'm looking for: a nice cave to do our eco survey."

Hassan bounced on his toes. "You think the cave will have bats?" he asked. "I'd love to see a bat."

Chapter 3

The Orb

Skeet frowned. This cave didn't look like it had ever been visited before. The rockfall near the opening was undisturbed. She took her head-torch from her backpack and snapped it on. Hassan watched carefully and did the same.

"Cave life is very special," Skeet said. "If we find something interesting, we should get top marks."

That would be excellent. Skeet wanted top marks all the time so that she could win a place at one of the best universities on Earth, but the trouble was that others had the same idea. Competition for academic first place was intense.

The cave was rugged inside, probably the remains of a lava tube.

Hassan's eyes were wide. "This is going to be the best!"

That encouraged Skeet. "Top marks are

waiting for us, Hassan. Let's look behind those rocks. There could be bats."

"Bats? Let's go."

They didn't find bats, but they did find a Prankster Orb.

Skeet and Hassan stood with their mouths open in front of the glowing silvery globe. It was the size of a basketball, and it hovered about a metre above the rocky floor.

Hassan spoke softly. "Did you know that the last person who found a Prankster Orb sold it for ten million dollars?"

Without taking her eyes off the orb, Skeet nodded. She also knew that Prankster Orbs were thought to have been scattered throughout the galaxy by a long-lost alien race called the Pranksters. Once opened, an orb vanished, never to be seen again.

Prankster Orbs could contain fabulous treasure or very advanced technology. Or they could instantly grant the finder amazing powers like telepathy or super strength. Other orbs, however, played a nasty trick on the opener. Skeet had read about people who'd turned into cabbages, or had their memories wiped, or who had just disappeared, never to be found again.

That's why most finders simply sold a Prankster Orb. Someone was always willing to pay big bucks to take the risk themselves.

"Is it real?" Hassan asked.

Skeet pointed her tablet at the orb and got an immediate response. "Sure is. We're rich."

"Why don't we open it?" Hassan said. "We could be richer than rich. We could become super rich."

Skeet frowned. "I don't know. What if we're turned into sea slugs or something?"

Hassan scratched his chin. "What are the chances of that?"

"Who knows? That's the problem."

"Here," Hassan said. "I'll open it. You can stand back."

"Uh-uh. No way. We'll both open it at the same time."

Together, they stepped up to the orb. "Ready?" Skeet said. "One, two, three!"

They reached out and touched the orb.

Instantly, the cave surrounds disappeared, and they were on a beach. Odd pink vegetation stretched away to a mountainous interior, while gentle green waves lapped the sand.

A huge alien faced them; he looked like an orange-and-white streaked crocodile. He had six legs, slicked black hair on his head, and lots of very sharp teeth.

He grinned at a terrified Skeet and Hassan and opened his mouth.

Chapter 4

Alien Island: A Live Reality Show

"At last!" the alien boomed. "Our final contestants are here!" He turned his head and looked up at the sky. "I'm your host, Jax Injelly! Welcome, everyone, to the lovely planet Blovia and *Alien Island*, the live-broadcast reality show where strange aliens are pitted against each other in fiendish tests and challenges! The prize for the winners? A luxury trip around the galaxy! The others? They remain here and go onto the next season of *Alien Island*!"

Skeet put an arm out and together she and Hassan backed away. They hit an invisible barrier. They were surrounded by a force field on all sides.

Jax looked at the sky again and pointed at Skeet and Hassan. "These two weird creatures are from a planet they call Mars! Isn't that cute? Say hello to the galactic audience, Mars creatures! I bet you like the gravity here; it's exactly the same as Mars!"

Skeet stared. "Who's he talking to?"

Hassan pointed at a horde of tiny hovering silvery objects. "Drones," he said. "I bet they're recording us. Or live streaming. Hard to tell."

Jax laughed. "Mars creatures. So primitive and so funny. Next, we have a pair from the far-off planet Plong! Welcome!"

Jax pointed. Not far away were two aliens that looked like large purple roosters with colourful throats and muscly arms and legs.

"Thanks, Jax," Green Throat said. "It's good to be here. We're looking forward to representing Plong and being the first team to get one thousand points."

"I love to hear confidence like that," Jax boomed. "And next to them are the pair from the planet Ooventing, halfway across the galaxy! Welcome!"

Skeet stared. These two looked like a bunch of sticks with three skinny legs underneath, like a tripod. On top they had an inverted bowl for a head. "We will reach one thousand points and win," one of the Ooventings said in a spindly voice. "We never lose. We will conquer."

Jax chuckled. "Let's wait and see about that. And our final pair is from the lovely planet Klock. Greetings, Klockians!"

These two were like giant green mushrooms. They had a row of eyes around their mushroom caps and many tiny legs like those of a centipede. "The others should admit failure now," one of the Klockians said. 'We'll win without even trying."

"You will fail," the taller Oovenfing said. "We will attain one thousand points before all others."

"We're the only winners," Green Throat said. "Give up now!"

Jax chuckled some more. He addressed the drones. "Looks like we're in for a crackerjack season everyone." He threw his arms wide. "Catch us next time for the first challenge round on *Alien Island*!"

He held his pose for a while, then he dropped his arms. A bunch of aliens that looked like knee-high beetles with multicoloured helmets scurried out of the jungle. Two carried a large chair and Jax collapsed into it. Another brought him a cool drink in a tall frosted glass. Another, some sunglasses.

Jax eyed Skeet and Hassan. "I guess you two want to know what's going on here, right?" Jax yawned, then explained: "We're beaming out to the Galactic Network and you're lucky enough to be part of one of its biggest shows. *Alien Island* is a legend in the industry."

"I don't care," Skeet snapped. "We want to go home."

"How come we can understand you?" Hassan asked Jax.

"The Universal Translator." He pointed at a drone. "I can understand you; you can understand me. It even works on written language. Don't ask me how, though. I can't even operate a bliphdax."

Hassan blinked. "A bliphdax?"

"Huh," Jax said. "Seems like there's no translation of bliphdax for you. Don't worry about it."

Skeet threw up her hands. "I don't care about bliphdaxes! I want to go home!"

"Sorry," Jax said. "No can do. Rules of the game. You win or you stay here. That's the way it is." One of the drones flew close to Jax's head. He listened to it and snapped his jaws. "Oh-ho! You two opened a Prankster Orb, right?"

"Maybe," Skeet said. "Why?"

"Well, every other contestant on the show is

here voluntarily, but if you opened a Prankster Orb you deserve what you get for being greedy."

"We weren't greedy," Skeet said.

"You could have left the orb alone," Jax pointed out. He snapped his jaws. "Anyway, you're here, you're part of the show, so you have to be first to reach one thousand points. If you do, you get to go home. If you don't, you go on to next season."

He rubbed a pair of hands together. "Get some rest. First challenge is tomorrow!"

The little beetles surged forward, and the force field dropped. Skeet, Hassan and the other contestants were herded towards a row of beachfront huts.

"Hey!" Skeet struggled. "Stop it!"

It was futile. The beetles were small, but strong. "Just go along with it," Hassan said. "We'll work something out."

The hut wasn't a prison, as Skeet had feared. It had two neat bedrooms and a living area. It even had a small kitchen with a fridge full of food that was promised to be fit for them.

Hassan went straight to it. "I'm dying of thirst," he said, and he held up a glass bottle with clear liquid in it. "I think it's water."

"Be careful," Skeet was about to say, but Hassan had already taken a mouthful.

"Not bad," he said. "It's like a cross between mango and strawberry."

Skeet tried the door that the beetles had closed behind them. It was locked. She dropped into a chair. "I don't like this," she said.

Hassan carried his bottle over to the chair opposite Skeet. "It looks like we don't have a choice. If we want to go home, we have to win."

"Win at what?"

"I guess we'll find out tomorrow."

Hassan opened his backpack and took out his tablet. He frowned at it. "Nothing. We're not connected. No beacon, no emergency messages home."

"Good idea to check though," Skeet said.

"I think we're going to need more than a few good ideas if we're going to win this thing," Hassan said.

Chapter 5

The First Challenge

In the morning, all the contestants were taken to the central arena: the main site for *Alien Island*. It had been cleared of trees and the area had been marked off with flags and ropes. Skeet wrinkled her nose. It smelled a bit like old seaweed.

Jax was there, surrounded by the tiny drones and attended to by his team of beetles. He waved a hand. "Over here, aliens. Hurry up."

"What's going on?" Skeet asked.

"We're laughing because aliens are so funny." Jax wiped a tear from his eye. "Weird creatures like you calling me, an ordinary old Blovian, an alien."

"Well, you are," Skeet said stubbornly.

Hassan nudged her. "Maybe it's how you look at it. At home, we'd be the ordinary ones. Out here though, it's different."

"The small one with head wings has a good point," Jax said.

"They're not head wings. They're ears," Hassan said.

"I like the way they stick out," Jax said. "It's very stylish." He clapped a pair of hands together. "All right, aliens. It's time for your instructions, so line up!"

Skeet was still fuming. "What if we don't want to?"

Jax's shoulders wiggled in a shrug. "It's up to you, but you'll finish last and won't score any points at all. Which means …"

"We won't get to go home," Hassan finished.

Skeet frowned. Finish last? She never finished last! "We'll just have to win, then," she said.

Skeet and Hassan joined the other pairs. The Klockians made rumbling noises. The Ooventings rustled. The Plongians put their heads together and whispered. Skeet narrowed her eyes. They looked like they were discussing tactics. They were serious.

Jax addressed the competitors: "We're just about ready to go live and the galactic audience will see all the action in real time. So, some last-minute things: the drones will capture all the action, so make sure you put on a good show. This scoreboard will hover over every challenge. It includes a fun countdown timer telling you how long you have left in the challenge."

Jax waved a hand, and a giant glowing display came out of thin air and hovered over them. The scoreboard was alive with graphics of each of the competing pairs. Next to them were numbers – all zeros.

"The Universal Translator also lets us read alien numbers?" Hassan said to Skeet. "I'm very impressed."

Skeet wasn't. She growled and crossed her arms over her chest.

One of the beetles scurried up to Jax. It was holding a big display tablet.

"We're nearly live," Jax said. He threw his hands wide and booming music played. "Welcome everyone to your favourite reality show, *Alien Island*! I'm your host, Jax Injelly. Get ready for a brand-new season of challenges, trials, thrills and spills. And remember – only one team wins a fabulous luxury trip around the galaxy and gets to go home as well!"

More music played, then Jax pointed at the brown expanse in front of them. "For today's challenge, teams need to get to the other side of the specially prepared arena. First team across gets top points, but bonus points are also awarded for finding little statues of me, Jax Injelly, and getting them to the finish line."

Hassan frowned. "What?" he said to Skeet. "Do we have to dig for these statues?"

Skeet sniffed. She had a bad feeling. "I don't think so."

Jax held up all his arms. "Aliens ready?" He dropped his arms. "Go!"

Chapter 6

Disaster

The Klockians were first to reach the arena and both creatures leaped straight into it. They landed with a splash and almost disappeared.

"Mud." Skeet groaned. "It's a mud pool."

The Plongians waded straight in and sank almost up to their waist feathers. They squawked in dismay while the Klockians bobbed up and ploughed forward, rumbling loudly.

The Ooventings, however, had stopped next to Skeet and Hassan. "You don't like mud either?" Skeet asked them.

The Ooventings twisted to look at her. "We are planning," the tall one said, and it sounded like trees in the wind. "Time spent planning is time well spent."

Then they were off. Skeet stared. The spindly creatures were running on top of the mud instead of sinking into it!

Hassan grabbed her hand and then jumped in, pulling her after him.

"Waargh!" Skeet cried and immediately discovered something she hated more than Mars dust. The mud was sticky, gluey and heavy, and came nearly up to her chest. The smell grew worse. It was definitely rotten seaweed. Her skin crawled as the mud enveloped her. "Ick! Ick! Ick!" she cried. "Get me out of here!"

"Come on," Hassan said. His face was grim. "We have to get moving."

Together, Skeet and Hassan slogged on. Skeet tried holding her nose to stop the smell, but her hands were covered with mud and it only made things worse.

Then Hassan disappeared.

One second he was struggling forward, the next he said, "Ouch!" and vanished under the mud.

Skeet panicked. "Hassan! Hassan!"

Hassan surfaced like a mud monster, but a happy one. He was holding a tiny object. He wiped his eyes. "I found a Jax statue!" he spluttered. "I tripped over it!"

"Bonus points!" she cheered, but the Ooventings were tiptoeing across the arena ahead of everyone, while the Klockians were ploughing away like small icebreakers. The Plongians weren't happy though. They hadn't made much more progress than Skeet and Hassan, and their feathers were caked with mud.

"Hurry," Skeet said to Hassan.

"Wait a minute." He groped under the mud. "There might be another statue down here."

Skeet bit her lip as she watched the other pairs forge ahead. "Leave it," she said. "We have to get to the other side."

The Ooventings were nearly across when Hassan wailed. "Oh, no!" he cried. "I dropped the statue!"

Hassan disappeared under the surface of the mud and then reappeared, blowing like a whale. "It's down there somewhere. Give me a minute."

He dived but was soon up again, dripping mud. "It has to be close."

A giant hooter went off. Jax's amplified voice rolled across the mud pool. "That's the end of the challenge! What a fantastic round that was! Just look at those scores!"

The giant scoreboard appeared, and Skeet's

heart fell. At the top, the Ooventings had 100 points. In second were the Klockians. The Plongians were third, and right at the bottom were Skeet and Hassan with no points at all.

"The Ooventings were sensational!" Jax bellowed. "A great effort by the Klockians, too, but the Plongians and those funny Marslings will have to do better next time! Especially if they ever want to go home!"

Hassan was covered with mud from head to toe. Skeet grimaced at the cold, gummy substance that was oozing everywhere.

Chapter 7

Puzzling

Skeet didn't sleep well that night. Even though she had showered and scrubbed, she could still smell the mud. Even her dreams were muddy.

When Skeet and Hassan fronted up for the next day's challenge, the sun was shining brightly and a soft breeze came off the ocean. The other pairs were smug. The Ooventings bounced up and down on their spindly legs, while the Klockians wobbled and chortled when they saw Skeet and Hassan. The Plongians pointed, ruffled their feathers and squawked.

"You two can't keep up with us," Yellow Throat said.

"You're on zero points, too, you know," Skeet snapped.

"Not for long," Green Throat said. "We're made to win."

Jax waddled over on his stumpy hind legs. "Now, now, save it for when we're live to air, which is in three, two, one and … Welcome to *Alien Island*, the most exciting, most challenging, most incredible reality show in the galaxy. I'm your host, Jax Injelly!"

The theme music blared, and Skeet looked at the arena fringed with pink-leaved trees. The mud had disappeared, and the arena floor was sandy. Four piles, each as big as a bus and covered with shimmering cloth, were evenly spaced around it.

The music died away and Jax swung around. "This challenge is one of my favourites! It's puzzle time!"

He pointed. "This is simple, really. Those piles are made from puzzle pieces. The first pair that can connect them all to make a complete picture wins top points. If no one completes a puzzle in the time limit, the pair with the most pieces in place wins." He snapped his fearsome jaws a few times. "Aliens ready?" He raised all his arms and then dropped them. "Go!"

Skeet raced for the nearest pile but was beaten by the Klockians. She veered around, made it to the next pile and, with Hassan's help, dragged off the shimmering cloth.

Hassan picked up the nearest puzzle piece. "These are the biggest jigsaw pieces I've ever seen." The piece he had in his arms was as big as a coffee table. "What's on it?"

It was all blue. Skeet groaned. "It's the worst jigsaw piece of them all. It's just sky."

Skeet lifted another piece. It was all blue as well. She put it on the sand next to Hassan's piece. They didn't fit together.

Hassan tilted his head back and shaded his eyes to look at the top of the pile. "This could take some time."

Eventually, the hooter sounded because the Klockians had finished. Their jigsaw was the size of a soccer pitch and showed a picture of Jax leaning against a brick wall and waving.

The Plongians only had a few pieces to go, and they stomped around unhappily. Their picture was of Jax in a flower garden.

The Ooventings had half a picture, but it was enough to tell that it was Jax waving to a crowd of admirers.

Skeet and Hassan had a dozen jigsaw pieces laid out and none of them connected to each other. They all showed blue, featureless sky except for one, which looked like an orange hand.

They scored zero points.

Hassan patted Skeet on the back. "Next time," he said.

Skeet shook her head. "I hope so."

All Skeet and Hassan had to do for the next challenge was weave the best-looking baskets out of a bunch of vines. Skeet was confident. How hard could it be to weave a basket?

When the final hooter sounded, though, she was hot, sweaty and frustrated. She had half a basket in her hands, but that half was so loosely made that it fell apart when she looked at it. When Hassan held up his basket, it was small, but it was neat with tightly woven strips of vine and a solid, square shape.

The trouble was that the other teams had gone much, much further with their weaving. The Ooventings had made four large baskets big enough to hide in, and each one had clever handles on the sides. The Klockians had done even better with a series of baskets like Russian dolls, fitting one inside the other. All of them were perfectly woven, even and tight.

The winners, though, were the Plongians. They only made one basket, but it was a work of art. On one side, they'd used different-coloured strips of leaves, and it was a dizzying maze of colour. But the other side was the reason their basket was the winner. It was woven to make an image of Jax Injelly smiling broadly.

Skeet had to admit that it was pretty well done. Hassan agreed.

Things went from bad to worse. The following day's challenge was to compose a song about Jax Injelly, and how amazing he was. The teams had a collection of musical instruments they could choose from, but none of them were familiar to Skeet. Hassan found a drum, but that was about as far as they got.

The other teams came up with clever songs that rhymed beautifully, even with the Universal Translator. They used the strange instruments to create sounds that were sometimes like hymns and sometimes like foot-stomping country-and-western music.

Skeet and Hassan's feeble effort didn't get much further than, "You can relax with Jax; he's a friend of Max."

Zero points, again. Skeet had high hopes when the next day's challenge presented the teams with familiar targets of the round concentric-circle type. She'd excelled in archery back home and she was sure that her aim was true.

But it wasn't an archery challenge; it was a throwing challenge. They had to throw small, orange blobby creatures, like water-filled starfish. The blobs loved being thrown, and cried, "Whee!" each time as they flew through the air before hitting the target with a high-pitched **Whacko!**

Skeet winced each time she picked up a blob out of the bucket. She felt like apologising, even though the little faces were excited and offered her encouragement each time. In the end, she shut her eyes as she threw, which didn't help at all.

At least Skeet hit the targets a few times, unlike Hassan. He still hadn't adjusted to Blovia's gravity, and his efforts were all over the place. "Sorry," he apologised, when they came last again. "The blobs kept sticking to my hand."

The Plongians were the best at blob throwing. They scored the maximum 100 points, with the other pairs also notching up decent scores.

Skeet and Hassan were given a score of zero again.

Skeet was crushed. She was last, at the bottom, with no hope of winning, ever. She had to do something.

Chapter 8

A New Plan

That night, Skeet and Hassan sat in their living room, exhausted. Hassan held a bottle of his now favourite mango-and-strawberry drink, but he'd hardly touched it. Skeet had made a toasted cheese sandwich, but she took one bite and suddenly wasn't hungry. It was very rubbery and, when she thought about it, it mightn't have been cheese at all.

The front door opened, and a team of beetles scurried in with baskets and boxes. Hassan waved to them. They went to the fridge and filled it.

"We'll never get home," Hassan said glumly.

"Don't be like that," Skeet said. "We'll find a way."

"I like Mars. It's my new home," Hassan said.

A beetle hurried up to him and interrupted. Hassan shook his head. "I'm okay, thanks."

Skeet stared. "Did that beetle just talk to you?"

"Sure. They're very helpful."

"I've never heard them talk."

Hassan scratched his head. "Maybe you haven't listened." He sighed. "Earth was so crowded. I miss the wide-open spaces of Mars. Did you know that you can just walk around, wherever you like? And you can use all the electricity you want to?"

Skeet rolled her eyes. "Of course I know that. Lots of solar panels on Mars mean lots of electricity."

"We had electricity rationing on Earth all the time. And water rationing. And food rationing. That's why we moved to Mars." He shook his head. "Earth had so many people competing for the same resources. It was getting really mean."

"That's it!" Skeet said. "If we're going to compete, we have to get meaner."

"Meaner? You're not thinking of cheating, are you?"

"Not cheating." Skeet picked up her sandwich and took a bite. "But we have to do something different."

Hassan scratched his head. "Like what?"

"Thinking differently. Thinking around corners. Thinking in a way no one expects. We have to get creative."

"Get creative. I like the sound of that."

"Get ready to follow my lead tomorrow, okay?"

"Yeah!" Hassan punched the air. "We're going to win!"

Skeet smiled. "We're not going to come last, that's for sure."

Chapter 9

Getting Creative

When the beetles came to collect them, Skeet bounced out of the hut ready for a new approach to the challenges. It was time to get creative.

Hassan was yawning when he joined her. He held out his hand for a high five. "We're winners today, right?"

"No more losing," she promised. "Just get ready for some top-level creativity."

The beetles directed them to the arena, where there were four low platforms. On each platform was a simple table. Skeet's stomach flip-flopped.

"Please, not another jigsaw," Hassan said.

"We're broadcasting live right now, folks," Jax said, addressing the drones that clustered overhead. "And our strange little creatures from

Mars are having a tough time, which is very entertaining."

Skeet put her fists on her hips. "We're trapped here playing stupid games and we keep losing and you think it's entertaining? That's awful!"

Jax laughed. "And that's the sort of emotion we bring to you, galactic audience. *Alien Island* is where you'll see it all – triumph, failure and heartache! Make sure you catch every episode!"

"Let's get on with it," Skeet growled.

Jax gestured and suddenly he was holding a small rectangular card. "See this?" he said. "Hundreds of these are on each table. Your challenge is to have the tallest structure when the final hooter sounds. And if you need more of these rectangles, just wave and our eager assistants will hurry them over to you!"

One of the Klockians rumbled loudly. "Mark us as winners right now. We are superior builders."

Green Throat gave a rude squawk. "We are certain to be the top constructors. We do this sort of thing every day."

The Ooventings leaned towards Skeet and Hassan. "Give up now, creatures from Mars," the tall one said. "You are poor competitors. Weep at our superiority."

Skeet rolled her eyes at such trash talk, but an idea was already forming. “We have to have the tallest structure when the hooter sounds?” she asked Jax.

“That’s right!” Jax said. “Be fast, be bold, but be careful, for these rectangles fall down easily.”

“House of cards!” Hassan said suddenly.

Jax stared at him. “What is this you say?”

“You want us to build a house of cards,” Hassan said. “That’s what we Martians call it.”

Jax roared with laughter. “That is so weird and strange, Mars creature!” He addressed the drones. “Remember, galactic audience, you heard it here first! House of cards!”

Skeet smiled. She’d been thinking hard and had an idea. It came from paying very close attention to what Jax had said.

Jax lifted all his arms. “Aliens ready? Go!”

Skeet and Hassan sprinted for the nearest table and this time they made it there first. The Klockians had to take the table on the left, a little further away.

On the hovering scoreboard, the clock was ticking down relentlessly. Skeet bit her lip. Her plan was all about split-second timing, so she had to keep an eye on how much time was left.

"You've done this before?" Skeet asked Hassan as they shuffled through the rectangles. They weren't exactly cardboard – more like stiff plastic, but not shiny or slippery.

He flexed one of the rectangles. "Sure, lots of times. Slow and steady wins the race."

He propped two cards against each other, then arranged two more next to them. Then he carefully placed a card horizontally on top. "There. We just repeat this over and over to build up and up."

Skeet eyed their competition. The other teams had worked out the same method as Hassan and were busy working on a bottom layer.

"Right," she said. "We need to build something solid. Something that won't fall down."

Hassan frowned. "Yeah, that's the aim."

"I mean really solid," Skeet said. "No need for much height, but lots of need for a really solid base."

Hassan took charge, and Skeet was glad for his steady hands. She was nervous, and her palms were sweating. The clock was counting down one digit at a time, bringing the end of the challenge closer and closer, when she'd have to spring into action.

Together they built a good layer, then backed it up with another. Skeet risked another glance at their competitors. The Ooventings were six layers high and working like machines. The Plongians were solid, with four layers, but were speeding up, with the Klockians close behind.

Skeet and Hassan worked carefully: card after card, layer after layer.

"Be careful," she whispered to Hassan as she leaned down. "But take off your shoes."

Hassan froze, two cards in his hands. He blinked. "What?"

"Hurry!"

She already had her shoes off. The clock was down to six seconds. "Look out!" she shouted.

Her aim was true. Her first shoe hit the Plongians' house of cards and it collapsed. They squawked in shock. Skeet's next shoe ruined the Klockians' structure and it tumbled.

She glanced at the clock. Three seconds left!

She took two steps to bring her closer and flung Hassan's shoe at the Ooventings' tower. They stood, unmoving, shocked at Skeet's assault, but this time she missed.

She grabbed Hassan's other shoe. Her last chance. She bit her lip, eased back, aimed and threw. The shoe hurtled past the amazed Ooventings and smacked right into their massive tower. It fell in a heap. At that instant, the hooter sounded.

Jax rushed up, the drone swarm following. "What's this? What's this?"

Skeet dusted off her hands. "We had to have the tallest structure when the hooter sounded, right?" She gestured at Hassan's modest two-level house of cards. "None of them have a taller structure than we do."

Hassan gave her a high five. "We got creative."

Jax threw back his head and snapped his jaws with delight.

Chapter 10

Villains

Jax signed off the episode with his usual hearty, "And make sure you catch the next exciting episode of *Alien Island*!" And then he turned to face the contestants. Six of them were outraged. Two were very pleased with themselves.

"Maximum points, no contest," Skeet said. She pointed at the hovering scoreboard. "We're on our way to the top."

The Plongians were squawking angrily. The Ooventings had put their heads together and were whispering. The Klockians muscled forward. "We must register our protest!" one of them said. "The Mars creatures interfered with our construction! They are villains!"

Jax tapped his jaw thoughtfully. "Every good reality show needs villains."

"We're not villains," Skeet said. "We just listened carefully to the instructions."

The Ooventings waggled. "Your construction was feeble and unambitious," the tall one said.

"It was the tallest when the hooter went," Hassan pointed out.

Jax waved at Skeet and Hassan. "They broke no rules," he said. "They won through creativity."

"Underhanded and unfair tactics," the Klockian said. "They must be penalised."

"I don't think so," Jax said. "Their cunning makes for great drama." One of the beetles rushed up and handed a tablet to Jax. "And the ratings say the audience loved it," Jax said. "They want more!"

The Klockians looked at each other. The Ooventings were still. The Plongians stopped squawking and conferred. Green Throat stepped forward. "We will change our tactics, then."

"Be warned, Mars creatures," the tall Ooventing said. "We are prepared to change our approach."

The Klockians weren't about to be left out. "We too look forward to the next challenge. We are famous for our cunning. We will win."

Skeet shrugged. "Bring it on."

"Sensational!" Jax clapped all his hands together. "A mid-season twist! This is perfect!"

The beetles herded the contestants back to their huts. Hassan chatted to them as they went, but Skeet hardly paid attention. She was thinking about how events had unfolded. They'd won a challenge, at last, but at what cost? The other teams were so angry! What would they do?

Hassan nudged her. "The beetles think your shoe throwing was funny. They thought you'd pulled off your feet and thrown them."

"Did you explain?"

"I told them that shoes are foot helmets. They laughed and were happy with that."

"Foot helmets." Skeet sighed. They were definitely a long way from home.

Chapter 11

The Chaos Round

"The classic maze challenge!" Jax announced the next day to the galactic audience, after the *Alien Island* theme music died away. He gestured at the arena, where a wall faced the competitors. "Inside are dead ends, false turns and plenty of likely but fruitless possibilities! The first team through the exit wins, and if no one makes it by the time the hooter sounds, whichever pair has gone furthest will win!"

"So, whoever's in front when time runs out is the winner?" Hassan asked.

"Exactly, small and strange Mars creature." Jax grinned at the drone cameras.

"And doesn't that open up all sorts of possibilities, galactic audience? And since it does, I'm going to give the pairs a couple of minutes to discuss how they're going to approach this amazing maze!"

Skeet grimaced. All their alien competitors were muttering to their partners and looking in Skeet and Hassan's direction. "This could be trouble," she said to Hassan. "How fast can you run?"

Hassan snorted. "Faster than those guys."

Skeet wasn't sure about that, but she nodded. "You sprint for the maze entrance and as soon as you're inside, keeping turning left."

"Left?"

"That's the standard tactic for beating a maze." She held up crossed fingers.

Hassan shook his head. "I'm more of a follow-your-nose guy. I have an excellent sense of direction, you know."

"Whatever. Go fast and I'll try to slow the others down."

"How? I don't think throwing shoes at them will work this time."

"I'll use my pet stobor."

"Stobor? What's that?"

"Never mind. Leave it to me," she said, as Jax clapped his hands together.

"Discussion time is over!" he announced.

"Aliens ready? Go!"

Skeet waved her hands over her head. "Wait! Wait! I think it's only fair that I warn our fellow competitors about my pet stobor."

Jax rubbed his ear. "Sorry, the Universal Translator didn't do anything with that. Stobor? What's a stobor?"

"It's a big predator from Mars. It has big teeth and fangs, with no natural enemies. We make pets out of them, and they're very loyal."

"What?" squawked Green Throat. "You have a pet?"

"And you brought it with you?" one of the Klockians asked.

"I need to tell you that it's very protective, and if you try to impede my progress through the maze, it could turn fierce."

"A big fierce creature?" the tall Ooventing said. "I heard something outside our hut last night. Did you turn your stobor loose?"

Skeet could have cheered. They totally believed her made-up story!

"It's hard to say. It's very elusive and only appears when you least expect it. It was over there a while ago." She pointed in the opposite direction to the maze and had trouble keeping a straight face when all the others turned to look.

"I didn't know you had a stobor," Hassan said.

Skeet swung around. Her mouth fell open. "You're not meant to be here! I bought you some time so you could get a head start in the maze!"

Yellow Throat heard. He spun around. "No, you don't!"

The Plongians leaped in front of Hassan and blocked his way. Skeet tackled one but a Klockian pulled her off. "Look!" she said. "The Ooventings!"

The spindly Ooventings had taken advantage of the mini riot and were sneaking towards the maze entrance. A Klockian galloped after them and bowled them over.

Things got messy after that.

When the final hooter went, no one had even made it as far as the entrance to the maze.

Skeet sat up and spat sand from her mouth. She dusted her hands off. Hassan rolled off one of the Plongians and climbed to his feet. Green Throat rolled over and glared at him.

"Hey now!" Jax bellowed. "That was unexpected! Unexpected but entertaining, right?" He addressed the drone swarm. "I'm afraid that round was a complete washout! No winners and no points for anyone!"

The scoreboard quivered and shook itself for a moment. A sad-face icon appeared before the unchanged scores flashed up.

“No one will be going home at this rate!” Jax said. “Which means plenty more excitement on *Alien Island*! Join us next time!”

When the drones shut down, Jax addressed the competitors. “Fantastic, all of you! Love it, love it, love it! If you keep this up, we’ll win a bucketload of awards, and you can all go on to next season, where you’ll face the Groozers.” He chuckled. “You’re going to love the Groozers. They’re fierce and they can really wallop you with their tentacles.”

Hassan hung his head. “We’re never going home.”

Chapter 12

From Hero to Zero

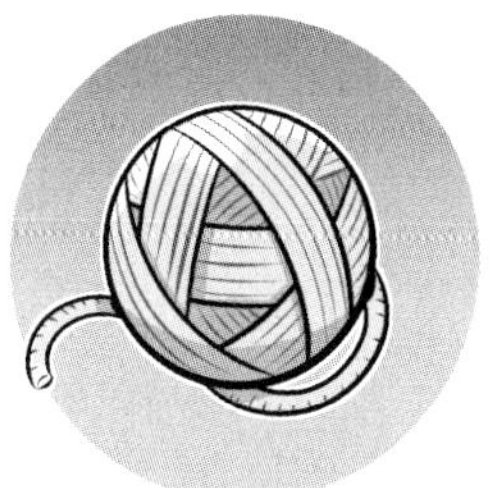

Over the next few days, every challenge fell apart as the teams spent most of their time stopping the others from winning instead of trying to win themselves.

When the pairs had to unravel a ball of string as big as a boulder, Skeet and Hassan had barely started when the Plongians rushed over and barged into their ball, rolling it to the far end of the arena. Skeet completely lost the end of the string she'd had in her hand.

The Plongians didn't have much time to gloat, however, as the Ooventings stole their ball and shoved it away. After that, it was a free-for-all, with pairs racing between retrieving their own ball and pushing any opponent's ball away.

Zero points all round.

Jax was the only happy one. This was spectacular viewing.

He addressed the exhausted, frustrated competitors. “I love what you’re doing,” he told them, “but remember: no violence. Bad for ratings. A bit of pushing and shoving is okay, but nothing more. After all, we want you all fit and ready for the next challenge. Whatever it’s going to be!”

So it went for five full days of challenges. At the end of it, Skeet was even more convinced she’d never see the open expanses of home.

She blinked. She was homesick for Mars; the place she couldn’t wait to leave! What was going on? Maybe there was no place quite like home.

The situation was so bad that even Hassan had lost his cheerfulness. “It’s gone from bad to worse, you know. First, there was only going to be one winner. Now, everyone loses.”

Skeet had to agree. With everyone battling against each other so brutally, they were all going to lose. She rubbed her chin. “What if there is a way for us all to win?”

Hassan brightened. “Is that possible?” he asked.

“It would need something special. It would have to start with trust,” Skeet said.

Chapter 13

A Different Plan

When Skeet asked Hassan if they could sneak out of the locked hut at night, she didn't think he'd shrug and say, "Too easy."

"Too easy? I thought there'd be some sort of hi-tech locking system in place."

"There is." Hassan grinned. "But that's what a master key is for."

He held up a swipe card. "One of the beetles gave it to me," he explained.

"Why?"

"They feel sorry for us. When I said I felt all cooped up, she gave it to me. It opens all the contestants' huts. Want to give it a try?"

Together, they crept through the shadows to the nearest hut. Skeet knocked gently and then unlocked the door with the master key.

Green Throat stomped up. "What's this?" he demanded. "Have you come to sabotage our efforts before the next challenge starts?"

Skeet held up her hands. "I just want to talk."

Yellow Throat appeared. "Hah! You wish to win at our expense!"

"What if we could all win the big prize? Plus we get to go home," Skeet said. "Let me explain."

It wasn't long before all the pairs were gathered in the Plongians' living room. Everyone was listening to Skeet.

"We want to go home," she said to the gathering. "And I have a plan that might work."

The tall Ooventing rattled and said, "Why did you come here in the first place?"

"It was an accident," Hassan said. "We opened a Prankster Orb."

Everyone reacted. The Plongians laughed, the Ooventings rattled and the Klockians rippled.

"And you ended up in a galaxy-wide reality show?" one of the Klockians said. "Those Pranksters. You never know what's going to happen if you open one of their orbs."

"What are you doing here?" Skeet asked her.

"With such a prize, we volunteered," the other Klockian said. "We also thought that we'd be famous."

The first Klockian shifted uneasily. “It doesn’t look like that’s going to happen now.”

The tall Ooventing rattled. “The luxury galactic tour is our goal, but we volunteered to be part of the show because we truly wanted to meet Jax. He was our idol.”

The other Ooventing sagged. “Sometimes it’s not good to meet your idols. The reality isn’t as good as the dream. His jokes are terrible.”

Green Throat clacked his beak. “We love travelling, so the tour-of-the-galaxy prize has great appeal.”

Yellow Throat shook his head. “The truth is that we wanted an *Alien Island* t-shirt. It wasn’t a good reason. Look at us now: trapped.”

Skeet seized the moment. “It seems to me that the *Alien Island* producers love it when we’re all competing hard against each other, but all that means is that there are no winners, only losers.”

“This is true,” the tall Ooventing said. “We are being exploited.”

“But what if there was a way for us all to become winners?” Skeet suggested.

There were lots of mutterings and gestures. “How?” a Klockian asked.

“By trusting each other,” Skeet said.

Chapter 14

Co-operation

In the end, the other pairs agreed to Skeet's plan. The Klockians and the Ooventings were keen, but the Plongians took some convincing.

When Jax saw them, he did his usual welcome to the galactic audience. Then he addressed the competitors. "A mental challenge this time, competitors!"

He gestured at a big, upright board. It was a grid of featureless tiles. Each tile was pearly white and about a metre square. The grid was 20 tiles wide and 20 tiles high.

"Each pair will take one of these pointers," Jax said, and the beetles scurried to hand over the small black cylinders.

"Laser pointers," Hassan breathed. "Cool."

"Press the button to indicate which tile you want flipped," Jax continued. "Your aim is to match the symbols on the reverse side of the tiles. If you match a pair, it's removed from the board and you have another turn. If you don't match a pair, then your turn is over. Whichever team has the most matches when the hooter goes is the winner!"

"It's a memory game!" Hassan said.

"Exactly!" Jax said. "And don't forget it!"

Hassan held the pointer in his hand. "We've got this."

Skeet nodded at the Ooventings and the Klockians. The Plongians stomped their feet a little, but Skeet hoped that meant that they were on board.

"The Mars creatures should go first," Jax said.

Hassan used the pointer and a red dot appeared on the bottom left-hand tile. He pressed the button, and the tile flipped over to reveal a triangle. Hassan moved the pointer so the dot landed on the tile in the top-left corner. It revealed three straight, vertical lines.

"No match!" Jax bellowed, as the tile flipped back to show its blank face. "Next!"

The Ooventings were next. Their first-choice tile revealed a triangle. They hesitated and put their heads together. Their red dot hovered over a nearby tile and they were about to press the button when Skeet waved her hands over her head. They looked at her. Skeet gestured: across, across, across, then down, down, down until the dot was resting on the bottom-left tile. Thumbs up.

The tile flipped and both triangles vibrated, glowed and rose out of the board.

"A match," Jax said slowly. "Not bad at all. You get another turn."

As the challenge went on, the pairs helped each other. The Klockians leaned this way or that to indicate a matching tile. The Plongians pointed. The Ooventings jumped up and down.

Throughout the challenge, Skeet kept an eye on the scoreboard. Skeet and Hassan were far behind, so they needed lots of points to catch up.

When the hooter went, Jax jumped. "Look at that!" he said when he addressed the camera drones. "The Mars creatures have won!" He snapped his jaws. "And isn't that amazing! They're now on equal points with all the other teams! A four-way tie!"

When he signed off, he put his hands on his hips. "I think there's something funny going on here," he said. "And I'm not sure I like it."

Chapter 15

The Final Round

Hassan came back from talking to a beetle. "We could be in trouble," he said to Skeet.

She sat up straight. "But it's going so well and we're so close."

"The beetles saw the Plongians having a secret conversation with Jax. They might betray us and go for the win themselves."

Skeet slumped. "Oh, no." She put her head in her hands. "We trusted them."

"It could be nothing," Hassan said. "They might have just been complaining. Those Plongians are good complainers."

The next day was the hottest day since they'd been on *Alien Island*. The air was already toasty at dawn when Skeet rolled out of bed after a nearly sleepless night. She went and stood by the window that looked out over the sea. Gentle waves broke on the beach and tall pink trees swayed in the breeze.

She was troubled. For the plan to work, the pairs needed to work together perfectly.

Hassan joined her at the window. "It's really pretty here, you know," he said.

"It is," Skeet replied.

"But I want to go home," Hassan said.

At the arena, for what Skeet hoped would be the final challenge, four brightly coloured wooden circles were placed in the corners of a square. On each circle was a pile of something that Skeet couldn't quite make out.

Jax waited until they arrived, then eyed all the teams. "I still don't know what's going on and I still don't like it, but the galactic audience seems to." He snapped his jaws slowly. "Anyway, look at the scoreboard."

The scoreboard appeared overhead. "Any of you can win and go home if you just want it badly enough, right?" He gestured and the camera swarm appeared. "It's showdown time!" he declared. "It's winner take all! It's everyone for themselves in what could be the final challenge for this season of *Alien Island!*"

Skeet waved to the other pairs. They waved back. But were the Plongians a little slow to respond? Skeet's palms were sweating.

Jax continued. "This challenge is a classic," he said. "It's simple, but it tests who really wants to win. Each pair has an equal number of seashells to begin with. When the starting hooter sounds, steal as many shells from your opponents as you can. When the final hooter sounds, whichever pair has the most shells wins the challenge, a hundred points and the grand prize of a luxury galactic tour!"

Jax leaned close to the contestants. In a low voice, he said, "And, of course, if you win you don't have to stay here and go on to the next season. You get to go home."

Skeet's heart pounded. She wanted badly to go home, so this was it. There was no turning back.

Jax straightened and chuckled to himself. "And I've added a little twist to this challenge, just for fun. Any pair that doesn't move off their circle will be disqualified and lose all the points they've accumulated! Now, that should be extra motivation, right?"

Skeet grimaced. When Jax described the

challenge, she'd thought that all the pairs needed to do was nothing! If they just stood there and waited, they could have all ended up on equal points and gone home.

Hassan scratched his head. "Looks like he wants a good show. Let's give it to them."

"You want to give up our co-operation plan?" Skeet asked.

"Nope," he said and whispered his idea to her.

Jax snapped his jaws. "Oh, I'm looking forward to this one! Aliens ready? Go!"

The pairs took up their positions and stood uncertainly for a while. Jax waved and bellowed. "Don't just stand there! We want action!"

Hassan nudged Skeet. "Grab a shell," he said. When she did, they held them over their heads, getting the attention of the other pairs. It took a moment, but they clearly understood. Each pair found two shells and held them up.

Hassan and Skeet trotted clockwise to the next circle and added their shells to the Plongians' circle. The Plongians had left by then and added their shells to the Ooventings' circle. The Ooventings had done the same to the Klockians, who had made it to Skeet and Hassan's circle and plonked their two shells down.

Everyone was even again.

Hassan waved his hands and the pairs were off, empty-handed, back to their own circles.

"Cut it out!" Jax bellowed. "You're supposed to steal from other people, not give yours away!"

"You didn't say we couldn't!" Skeet called, and Hassan's instructions kept the pairs moving like a complicated dance routine.

When the hooter went, the piles of shells were exactly equal. Overhead, the scoreboard lit up and everyone had reached 1000 points.

Skeet and Hassan sprinted to the centre of the arena and joined the others, who were jumping up and down, wobbling and rustling.

"We heard you had a secret meeting with Jax," Skeet said to Green Throat. "We thought you were going to betray us all."

"Hah!" he said. "We pretended so he'd think everything was going to end as he wanted. Instead, he lost."

Jax came waddling over. "Hold on! I'm the host of this show and I say that challenge doesn't count. It was a fraud and none of you win. In fact, you're all back to zero and have to start again!"

Skeet's heart fell, but at that moment a troop of beetles skittered over and handed Jax a tablet and headphones. “What?” Jax said to the tablet. “Are you sure? Really?” He snapped his jaws a couple of times. “Well, that’s sensational!”

He tossed the tablet and headphones to the beetles. “Forget everything I just said! That was the Galactic Network Big Boss. She said that this has been the top-rated season of *Alien Island* ever, and it really took off when you started your co-operative approach. You’re all winners and you’ll all be going home!” He clapped his hands together. “I’m sure glad that I came up with this twist. Jax Injelly, you’re a genius.”

“We’re going home,” Skeet crowed.

“As soon as we get home, I’m going to have a milkshake,” Hassan said. “And eat a whole box of cereal. And go and look at those giraffes.”

“I’m going to spend some time really getting to know Mars,” Skeet said. “Hiking, looking into its history, getting to know the ins and outs of those giraffes. Want to help?”

Hassan grinned. “Count me in.”

Skeet tapped her chin thoughtfully. “But before we go home, what about taking a little luxury trip around the galaxy?”

Hassan high-fived her. “Great idea!”